A Wild No...
Griswo... Newm...
The ... the poached egg

THE CASE
OF THE
POACHED
EGG

DISCARDS

BY
ROBIN NEWMAN

ILLUSTRATED BY
DEBORAH ZEMKE

MISS RABBIT'S HOUSE

GOOSE CREEK

COW BARN

COW PASTURE

MILKY WAY

PIG PEN

CHICKEN COOP

HOT DOG'S HOUSE

ED'S HOUSE

OLD BARN

MFI HEADQUARTERS

STABLE

ED'S FARM
38.9517° N, 92.3341° W
PROPERTY OF MFI

MFI

Captain Griswold

MFI

Detective Wilcox

Boys and girls, this case is about a poached egg on Ed's farm.

Over 100 animals live on this farm. Most work. Some horse around. Others steal.

That's where I come in. My name is Detective Wilcox. I'm a policemouse.

The boss is Captain Griswold. We're MFIs, Missing Food Investigators. It's our job to investigate cases of missing food.

Whatever the food, whatever the crime, we make the bad guys do the time.

Farmer Ed's Big Speggtacular was coming up and you could be sure of one thing: trouble. It could hatch at any time.

It was 10:00 Tuesday morning. The captain and I were working the early shift when we got our first call.

Case File #1156:
The Poached Egg

10:00 am, Headquarters

"Headquarters. Wilcox, here."

"This is Henrietta Hen. My precious Penny is missing."

"Did she fly the coop?" I asked.

"Oh no! She can't fly."

"Did she run away?" I probed.

"Oh no! She can't run."

"Can't fly or run? I've never heard of a chicken who couldn't cross the road."

"She's not a chicken."

"Not a chicken? What is she?"

"An egg."

I sure had egg on my face. "Are you sure she's gone?"

"Yes, Detective. I always count my chickens before they hatch."

"We're on our way!" I said.

"Captain, we've got a Code 0, a poached egg."

The captain held up a pot of water.

"Not poached as in boiled," I said, "poached as in stolen!"

We jumped into our cruiser and flew to the coop.

3

The Crime Scene

10:30 am, Chicken Coop

It was a boc boc here and a boc boc there.

"Boc boc," cried Henrietta. "Over here!"

"Detective Wilcox and Captain Griswold, MFIs," I said, flashing my badge. I pulled out my pen and notepad. "What happened, ma'am?"

"This morning I overslept, most unusual for me! When I woke up, Penny was gone from the nest and there was this instead."

"Egg-napping," I whispered to the captain.

"Do you recognize the handwriting?" I asked Henrietta.

"No," she sniffled.

"We'll need a picture of the missing egg," I said.

"That's my pretty Penny on the poster!" The captain sketched Penny's likeness.

"Who's been in the coop?" I asked.

"Nobody but us chickens . . . and Gabby Goose and Colonel Peck."

Hmm. . . a goose and a rooster in a hen house. Was fowl play involved? "What was Gabby Goose doing here?"

"She wanted to talk turkey about the Big Speggtacular. Holy cow! That goose could talk the ears off a donkey."

"Colonel Peck paid a visit, too?"

"He was searching for his missing kernels of corn. The colonel is ALWAYS losing his kernels. Detectives, I'm worried Penny could hatch at any time," clucked Henrietta.

"If we don't find Penny fast," I whispered to the captain, "she might end up in an omelet. Or worse, in a bucket of fried chicken!"

We had to scramble on this case. Scramble before we had scrambled eggs indeed.

Suspects & Clues

11:00 am, Cooped Up

We were dusting for prints when Colonel Peck strutted in.

"Detectives, am I glad to see you! Two kernels of corn are missing from my feed! It may not seem like much, but every kernel counts!"

"You can file a missing kernel report down at the station," I said.

"I just might!"

"Henrietta mentioned you were here yesterday. When was this?"

"Some time after the cows came home. Couldn't find a single kernel so I left and headed over to Miss Rabbit's. She invited Porcini and me over for carrot cake and a game of Go Fish."

"Was anyone lurking around the coop?" I asked.

The colonel lowered his voice. "I know I'm walking on eggshells, but I'll just come out and say it: Gabby Goose and Henrietta were squawking."

"About what?"

"Some silly squabble about Henrietta's eggs always taking first prize. Gabby's eggs finish second every time. No contest!"

"Was Gabby behaving suspiciously?"

"Like an odd duck—even for a goose! She was hanging around Henrietta's nest."

The captain had that "if-you-know-anything-you'd-better-spill-the-beans" look.

"Have you seen this?" I asked.

"No, what is it?"

"A ransom note for Penny. Recognize the

handwriting?" I grilled him.

"Nope, but I'd bet my tail feathers scribbling that bad could only be made by a silly goose."

"Isn't it interesting the thief wants to be paid in corn?" I hoped his reaction might give me a clue.

"Exactly! Geese eat corn. Lots of it!" The colonel flapped off in a huff.

"So do roosters," I whispered to the captain, who was clearly thinking the same thing.

The captain snapped photographs of the crime scene while I collected feather and eggshell samples. This case was going to be a hard-boiled egg to crack. A hard-boiled egg indeed.

Eggs-amining the Evidence:
12:00 pm, Cow Crossing on Milky Way

A herd of cows was crossing the road to get to the udder, I mean other, side. I pulled out my emergency supply of cheese donuts and tossed one to the captain.

The captain munched while I studied the prints from the crime scene—chicken, rooster, and goose prints. No surprises here! It was the same story for the feathers. So far, the evidence wasn't helping at all.

I took a bite of my donut. One, two, three bites, chew. The captain bit into his. One, two, three bites, chew. Cheese donuts always helped us think.

Something was strangely familiar about the shape. And then it hit me!

"Holy cannoli, captain! The ransom note! See this." I pointed. "Every letter e is backwards."

The captain's whiskers twitched and he grinned his "we're-on-to-something" smile.

"We'll need to see everyone's handwriting," I said. "Let's start with Gabby Goose once these cows MOOOOO-ve out of the way. MOOOOO-ve out of the way indeed!"

Suspect #2

12:30 pm, Gabby's Nest at Goose Creek
We parked in front of the creek.
"There's Gabby!" I
pointed at the goose wading
in the water with some
ducks.

"HONK!" The captain beeped.
"HONK!" Gabby replied.
"Detectives, you won't believe this, but I just
had my afternoon swim. Well, it was supposed
to be my morning swim, but I overslept, so

my morning swim became my
afternoon swim, which isn't
terrible, but what happens to my
evening swim? Does that become
my afternoon swim, or do I still
call it my evening swim. . ."

12

"Excuse me, Gabby, but. . ."
I started to say when Gabby
interrupted.

"And have you
heard the horrible
news?" Gabby gabbed
on. "I was talking to the ducks, who
heard it from the cows, who heard it
from the sheep, who heard it from
the chickens. Only a rotten egg could do such a
thing! Poor Penny!"

"Colonel Peck mentioned that you were at
the coop yesterday," I said.

"I stopped by for a quick hello. Well, it
started as a quick hello, but of course, a quick
hello became a hen party,
but not just a hen party
because I'm a goose, so
it was a hen and goose
party, and . . ."

No wonder this goose was called Gabby.

"Did you notice anything suspicious?"

"One thing! Colonel Peck was as sour as vinegar. His feathers were all in a ruffle about his missing kernels," Gabby squawked. "Missing kernels and now a missing egg! Could somebody be making corn bread?"

"Or getting a rival out of the way!" I said. "Word around the farm is that with Penny out of the picture, Gertie is a sure winner at the Speggtacular."

"My gorgeous Gertie would win no matter what!" honked Gabby, "but I do feel bad for Henrietta."

"Can you take a gander at this?" I asked.

The captain handed Gabby the ransom note.

If you ever want to see your precious Penny again, bring five bags of unmarked corn to the stable at 10:00 am. tomorrow. Come alone!

"Oh no!" Gabby wailed. "I knew it was bad, but I didn't realize it was ransom-note-bad."

"Do you recognize the handwriting?"

"No, but a goose would never write such chicken scratch."

The captain handed me a printout of Gabby's RAP sheet, a record of arrests. She had a couple of corn priors but was clean otherwise.

Next the captain handed me a card and gave me a wink. I knew the plan.

"Gabby, would you mind signing this card for Henrietta? We'd like to cheer her up. Maybe you should sign it Gabby Goose so she knows it's from you."

"There's only one goose named Gabby on this farm."

"How about 'love Gabby'?" I suggested.

"Great idea!"

The captain held the card next to the note. He shook his head. No match. We had come up with a big goose egg.

Back in the squad car, the captain spread out a map of the farm.

"Look here, captain!" I pointed. "Miss Rabbit has such keen ears, she may have heard something. Nothing peeps without her noticing. And Porcini's pigsty is just across the road. He could have seen something."

The captain nodded with his "let's-catch-this-rat" look. We had to hurry before our goose was cooked. Cooked well done indeed.

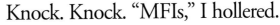

Knock. Knock. "MFIs," I hollered.

"Door's open. Come on down," shouted Miss Rabbit.

We slid down the rabbit hole and landed in the kitchen.

"Detectives, how nice of you to drop in," said Miss Rabbit. "Would you like some carrot cake?"

"This isn't a social call," I announced. "Penny has been egg-napped." I pulled out my notepad and started taking notes when I noticed Miss Rabbit was wearing her pajamas.

"Did we wake you?" I asked.

"I'm normally up with the chickens, but this morning I overslept. I didn't hear Colonel Peck crow."

Hmm. . . Henrietta and Gabby had also overslept. Now that I thought about it, I hadn't heard the rooster crow either.

"Have you seen anyone hanging around the coop?"

"Just that cocky rooster."

The captain tapped me on the shoulder. Carrots, flour, milk, vanilla, and an empty egg carton were on the kitchen counter. *EGGS!!??!!*

"Are those cake ingredients?" I asked.

"Yes. Have a slice. It's delicious."

Could Miss Rabbit be our egg-napper? Needing an egg for her carrot cake would certainly be a motive.

The captain pointed to the garbage pail. Eggshells! This case had just gone from the frying pan into the fire.

The captain compared the eggshells to the sketch he'd made of Penny and shook his head. What a relief! None of those shells were Penny. We still needed a writing sample from Miss Rabbit. Everyone was a suspect until Penny was home safe and sound.

"Would you mind signing a card for Henrietta? We're hoping to cheer her up."

"Oh! I'll just bring her some carrot cake," Miss Rabbit offered.

"A note is more personal. Besides, I doubt she'd eat anything made with eggs."

"You're right!" Miss Rabbit agreed.

The captain pulled out the ransom note and placed it next to Miss Rabbit's sample. He shook his head. No match here.

This case was turning into a wild goose chase. A wild goose chase indeed.

2:45 pm, Porcini's Pen

"Porcini," I called out, rapping on his door, "let the MFIs in, or we'll huff and we'll puff!"

"Detectives," Porcini oinked. "What can I do for you?"

"Henrietta's egg, Penny, is missing," I said.

"Was Penny taken or did she run away?" asked Porcini.

"An egg can't run!" I protested.

"Well, I've seen a lot of them scramble!"

"Speaking of scramble," I grilled, "have you had scrambled eggs recently?"

"Not recently enough!" Porcini snapped.

Could he have taken Penny for breakfast and written the ransom note to throw us off the trail of egg shells?

The captain had that "you're-in-hot-water-if-you-don't-start-squealing" look.

"What did you eat for breakfast?" I gave Porcini the third degree.

"You won't believe this, but I missed breakfast. I feel faint. I could use a cheese donut."

The captain tossed him one.

"Have you seen anything unusual at the coop?" I pressed.

"You mean like an egg-napper? Nope. Just clucking chickens and the colonel counting his kernels."

The captain pointed to a corner of the pen.

"Did you write this?" I demanded.

"With my own two hooves!" said Porcini.

"Nuts!" I murmured to the captain. So far everyone had a motive, but nobody's handwriting matched.

Back at headquarters, we pored over the evidence. One hour. Two hours. Three hours. The clock kept ticking. Day turned to night and night to day. With no clues, no plan for finding Penny, one thing was clear: our bacon was fried. Fried to a sizzle indeed.

Chapter 4

A Crack in the Case

9:00 am, Most Oval Contest, the barn

The next morning everyone eagerly waited for the contest to begin.

"Colonel, you wanted to file a missing kernel report? We'll need you to sign it." I held out the paper and a pen.

"Later! Right now I need to judge the contest."

The captain made his "that's-the-fishiest-excuse-I've-ever-heard" face.

I glanced at my watch and took one more peek at the ransom note. We had one hour until Henrietta was scheduled to make the ransom drop—five bags of unmarked corn.

"Captain, do you think the egg-napper will show up?"

The captain's whiskers twitched. He wasn't sure.

"Here they come!" I whispered to the captain.

The chicken and goose eggs wiggled, wobbled, and rolled in front of Colonel Peck. One lone turkey egg would not budge.

"That's one hard boiled egg." I nudged the captain.

Colonel Peck scribbled some notes and passed an envelope to Miss Rabbit.

"For the first time in the history of the Big Speggtacular, the winner is a goose egg. Congratulations, Gertie!" Miss Rabbit announced.

The crowd went wild. Gabby smiled, but wasn't egg-xactly egg-static. Something wasn't right.

The reporters gathered around Gertie and Gabby.

Rocky Raccoon, cub reporter for *The Daily Boc,* asked the first question.

"Gertie, what's it like being the first goose egg to win?"

"I'll answer that," offered Gabby. "Gertie is proud as a peacock. But winning isn't everything. It doesn't mean much when Penny is missing. Gertie is withdrawing from all other events. No questions, please."

"I thought you wanted to win," I said to Gabby.

"I do, but first we need to get Penny home safe. Any leads?"

"Not much," I admitted.

The captain pointed at the colonel. He was no spring chicken, but he sure could shake a tail feather when he needed to be somewhere in a hurry.

I rushed up to him. "Colonel, got a minute?"

"Look at the egg timer. Not one second to spare," huffed the colonel, flapping away.

"Wait! You dropped your scorecard," I shouted. But he was already on the fly.

I glanced at the card. "Captain, you need to see this."

We'd finally won the whole enchilada. The whole enchilada indeed.

Chapter 5

The Ransom Drop

10:00 am, The Stable

"Henrietta, over here!" I whispered.
The captain handed her five bags of
unmarked corn.

"If you need us, we'll be nearby.
Holler the secret code. Backup is
on the way."

"Boc," Henrietta clucked.

The captain and I hid inside a horse stall. Then we waited. And waited. And waited.

Just when the captain started to snore, a voice crowed, "Put the corn down and slowly walk away."

"Not without my Penny," squawked Henrietta.

From one of the stalls, an egg slowly rolled toward her.

"Penny, baby!" cried Henrietta, hugging her egg.

Now that Penny was safe, Henrietta was madder than a wet hen. I'd never seen steam come off a chicken before.

"Come on out and show your feathers!" she yelled. "You big chicken!"

"Think you can henpeck me?" the voice jeered.

From the shadows, our egg-napper came into view.

The bill.

The wattle.

And the comb.

"Colonel Peck! We knew it was you!" I accused. "Instead of crowing this morning, you poached Penny and left the ransom note. You figured everyone would be asleep. Nobody would suspect a rooster, right? And it worked, except for one thing."

The captain handed the colonel the ransom note.

"See the letter e's. They're all backwards. We took writing samples from everyone. Nobody else writes their e's backwards."

"How did you know that I did?"

"You dropped your scorecard."

"Well, one chicken and two little mice aren't going to stop me," sneered the colonel.

I thought he might have a point, when I remembered we had backup. I shouted the secret code.

"The eagle has landed!"

Nothing happened. Where was our backup? Did they chicken out? Without backup, we were sitting ducks. Sitting ducks indeed.

"The eagle has landed! The eagle has landed!" I yelled even louder.

Gabby, Porcini, and Miss Rabbit stormed
into the stable.

"Maybe one chicken and two little mice can't stop you, but a very angry goose, pig, and rabbit will!" I said. "You're coming with us, Colonel Peck!"

"I just wanted my corn back and maybe a little extra. It's not like I laid an egg."

"Colonel, where you're going to be cooped up, you'll never to have to worry about missing kernels again."

This case was finally looking sunny-side up. Sunny-side up indeed.

Chapter 6

A Spectacular Speggtacular

11:00 am, Prettiest Egg Contest, the barn

"Captain, there they are!" I shouted. Penny and Gertie wiggled, wobbled, and rolled in front of Judge Porcini.

Porcini handed Miss Rabbit the envelope.

"Ladies and Gentlemen," said Miss Rabbit, "The winner of the prettiest egg contest is. . . ."

A loud CRACK rang out. Then another. And another.

"Looks like someone is chickening out of the egg contest," I told the captain.

"Penny!" cried Henrietta.

"Mama?" chirped Penny.

The crowd was egg-static as Penny took her first steps.

"The winner of the prettiest egg contest is Gertie!" Miss Rabbit announced.

Gabby looked like she had just laid a golden egg.

"At long last, a spectacular Speggtacular!" I cheered.

12:00 pm, Case Closed.

Boys and girls, the case you've just read was about one poached egg and one rotten egg, who turned out to be a greedy rooster.

Every day food goes missing on this farm. Sometimes it's lost. Sometimes it's stolen. Sometimes it runs away. And sometimes it might even hatch.

With all these animals, you can be sure of one thing: trouble. It's sure to crop up. These are the cases for MFIs.

Whatever the food, whatever the crime, MFIs make the bad guys do the time.

No eggs, chickens, geese, or roosters were harmed during the writing of this story, but that doesn't mean there wasn't a bit of fowl play.

Heartfelt thanks from RN (alias: Snack Snatcher) to special agents Liza Fleissig and Ginger Harris-Dontzin, for their endless support and encouragement.

EVIDENCE